WHO'S THAT GIRL?

GET READY FOR
MORE GABÍ!

GET READY FOR GABÍ!

WHO'S THAT GIRL?

by **Marisa Montes**

illustrated by **Joe Cepeda**

> That's Gabí. As in Ga-BEE. With an accent. Not Gabi. 'Cause that's the way she likes it. Oh, and it does NOT rhyme with blabby! And she does NOT talk too much!

A
LITTLE APPLE
PAPERBACK

SCHOLASTIC INC.

New York   Toronto   London   Auckland   Sydney
Mexico City   New Delhi   Hong Kong   Buenos Aires

No part of this work may be reproduced, stored in a retrieval system, or transmitted in any form or by any means, electronic, mechanical, photocopying, recording, or otherwise, without written permission of the publisher. For information regarding permission, write to Scholastic Inc., Attention: Permissions Department, 557 Broadway, New York, NY 10012.

ISBN 0-439-47521-X

Text Copyright © 2003 by Marisa Montes.
Illustrations copyright © 2003 by Scholastic Inc.
SCHOLASTIC, LITTLE APPLE and associated logos are trademarks and/or registered trademarks of Scholastic Inc.

12 11 10 9 8 7 6 5 4   3 4 5 6 7 8/0

Printed in the U.S.A.   40

First paperback printing, September 2003

The display type was set in Circus Mouse.
The text type was set in Espirit.
Book design by Joyce White

To my brother
and to everyone who
loves their siblings
and wants to protect them.
— M. M.

To the Licanos
— J. C.

Acknowledgments

Special thanks to Janine Elya, Carolyn Elya, and Ethan Williams for providing me with lots of fresh third-grade fun and ideas.

Another special thanks to my cousin Lourdes I. Montes, M.D. for being my medical consultant and to my aunt, Dr. Carmín Montes Cumming, for being my Spanish consultant and supporter. A big thanks to my uncle, Bob Cumming, for all your help. And thanks to my husband and *very best friend,* David Plotkin, for your constant love and support.

Thanks to my critique group, Susan Middleton Elya, Raquel Victoria Rodríguez, and especially Corinne Hawkins, for your support, enthusiasm, and terrific ideas on the resolution of the conflict.

And an extra big thank-you to my editor, Maria S. Barbo, for your willingness to brainstorm with me, for your guidance, and for your insightful suggestions.   — M. M.

CONTENTS

UNO
CHAPTER 1
GABÍ THE GREAT!

"Watch out, World!" I yelled from high above my room.

I was jumping on my bed, wearing my red cowgirl boots. My wavy hair bounced as I jumped. High. Higher. *Higher still!*

"I'm Maritza Gabriela Morales Mercado — also known as —"

I hopped off the bed and flung a red beach towel around my shoulders like a cape.

"*¡La Gran Gabí!* Gabí the Great!"

I took my favorite pose: fists on my hips, boots slightly apart.

"That's Ga-BEE, with the accent on BEE. 'Cause that's the way I like it!"

Like my favorite superhero, Dragon-Ella, I was ready to fight crime and stamp out evil.

"Bullies be warned! Get ready for Gabí! *¡Gabí está aquí-ííííí!*"

Just then, my black-and-white cat, Tippy, wandered in the open door.

Quick as anything, I tied a red scarf around his neck. It flowed behind him like bright bat wings. (If you haven't noticed yet, my favorite color is red.)

As soon as the scarf touched his neck, he magically became my super-*gato* sidekick.

"And here is El Tiperú!" I held El Tiperú up in the air and swished him around. He was flying!

The moment I set him on the floor, El Tiperú zipped out the open door.

"Yes!" I cried, racing after him. "We're on the trail of bad guys!"

Just as I rounded the corner into the family room, someone grabbed me from behind and pinned my arms to my sides.

"*¡Te agarré!* Now I got you!" said a low voice. "Let's see how *great* La Gran Gabí *really* is!"

¡Ay, ay, ay! It was the Dreaded Abu-Della, Wicked Woman of the West! (Actually, it was just Abuelita, my grandma. But Abu-Della sounds more like an evil villain.)

Abu-Della tied my hands behind me.

Her dark eyes shone with evil!

Now what?

All I had was my secret weapon, my trusty pair of red boots. And Abu-Della was eyeing them! She knew they were the source of all my power.

¡Caracoles! Yikes!

As Abu-Della grabbed for my boots, I made my move. I kicked my right foot, and *off* flew my boot! It whizzed into the air, hit the carpet, and bumped her on the leg.

But that's all I needed. One touch from my boot, and my enemies drop. Abu-Della flopped to the floor.

She wouldn't budge — for now.

I broke free of my ties and jumped up.

"Aha!" I cried. "How *great* is Gabí the Great *now*?"

Then I stuck out my rear for a hip-wiggle victory dance, when —

Something jumped onto my back, screaming, "*¡Aaaaaa-iiiiii-eeee!*" It could only be Abu-

Della's winged monkey (otherwise known as my four-year-old brother, Miguelito).

I fell to the floor. I couldn't move.

"Got-you!Got-you!Got-you!" he said in a squeaky voice. The winged monkey smushed my cheek into the carpet!

I stopped squirming and played dead. Maybe I could trick the monkey into letting me go. I held my breath.

The winged monkey let go of my head. As soon as he sat back, I leaped up and tapped him with my boot.

"I'm free!" I shouted. "*Bien hecho*, El Tiperú! The world is safe from evil once more!"

I looked around for Tippy. "El Tiperú?"

"He's hiding," whispered the monkey. "He's under the couch."

"*Shhh!*" I said. "You're supposed to play dead. Anyway, El Tiperú *never* hides. He takes cover. Only wimps hide."

Miguelito tilted his head to get a better

look at Tippy. "Nope. I'm pretty sure he's hiding. See how —"

"*Shhh-hhh!* Put your head down."

"Nooo-ooo!" My brother shook his head. His shiny dark hair flopped back and forth. "I'm tired of playing dead. Why do I always have to be the *bandido*?"

"Because I said so. I'm the big sister, so I get to make the rules. You don't see Abuelita — I mean, Abu-Della — complaining, do you?"

I pointed at the still body of Abu-Della. Just then, the still body sat up.

"*Ay, Gabrielita, es tarde,*" she said. "It's getting late, and I promised your *mami* I'd make dinner tonight."

Abuelita spoke to us in Spanish. She's visiting us from Puerto Rico and that's the only language she knows.

But that's okay because my family *always* speaks Spanish at home. It's Mami and Papi's rule, so we'll never forget it. They want Miguelito and me to speak really good English, too, but we get lots of that at school.

"Ohhhh, ok-kaaayyy." I hung my head.

"*Mira*, Gabrielita, look." Abuelita waved her arm. "See, no bad guys. *El mundo* is safe from evil once more! All because of La Gran Gabí and El Tiperú!"

I grinned. "Yeah!" I stomped my boot.

"*Ahora*," said Abuelita, "why don't you *niños* go out and play while I start dinner? Your *mami* and *papi* will be home from work soon."

Miguelito bounced on his toes. We both yelled, "*Yeay!*"

Then I grabbed his hand and we ran out to get our bikes.

DOS
CHAPTER 2
MYSTERY NEIGHBORS

I rode my glittery red bike toward the spooky old house down the street.

Miguelito pedaled beside me on his big blue plastic tricycle. It made a huge racket as he pumped his short legs, trying to keep up.

As we rode, I thought about Abuelita. She had surprised us with a visit last month. We didn't know how long Abuelita would stay, so I was spending as much time with her as I could. I hoped she'd never leave.

Before we reached the end of the block, I slowed down and gulped.

Across the street, the old house filled the

sky. Purple and orange paint chipped off its wooden walls. The right corner had a creepy tower with windows all around. And the big front door was wide open, like a mouth ready to gobble up someone.

The kids at school thought the old house was haunted. Mami always said it wasn't. But Miguelito and I weren't so sure.

We stared quietly for a moment. Then Miguelito pointed to a big truck.

"*¡Mira!¡Mira!¡Mira!*" he yelled. "*¡Un camión!*"

I jumped. "*Shhh!* We have to be very *quiet.*"

Miguelito put a pudgy finger on his lips. "*Shhh, silencio,*" he whispered.

I looked at the truck. The back doors were open. A big old ramp ran from the back of the truck to the street.

Two huge men were carrying a couch down the ramp.

It must be a moving van!

"A new family's moving in!" I shouted, forgetting to be quiet. I slid off my bike and did a happy hip-wiggle. "New neighbors might mean new kids!"

"And new kids could mean new friends!" Miguelito yelled back.

He hopped off his trike and bounced beside me like a ball of Silly Putty.

We've never had kids our age on our block before. All the other kids are much older.

We set our bikes under a mulberry tree, and I helped Miguelito cross the street. The closer we got to the huge spooky house, the harder Miguelito squeezed my fingers. That's what he always does when he's scared.

I glanced around. I didn't see any new neighbors. And there were no signs of kids. Lots of boxes were stacked on the lawn. But no toys or bicycles.

"Careful, kids," said one of the big men. "Don't get too close to the house. I heard

some chains rattling. Might be ghosts."
Then he laughed real loud.

Miguelito ducked under my arm and glued himself to my side.

I patted his head. *"Está bien, Miguelito,* he's just kidding . . . *I think."*

I stared at the dark windows of the tower. *Did something move up there?*

The two men kept going back and forth carrying boxes and furniture.

Then a third man came out of the house. He went up the ramp and walked down carrying a chair.

"Are you the new neighbor?" I asked.

"Nah, kid. I'm just one of the movers. The new owners aren't here yet. Real estate lady let us in."

"Oh," I said. "Do you know when they will move in?"

"Nope. Not my business." He put down the chair to wipe his sweaty face.

"Do they have kids?" Miguelito asked.

"You kids are full of questions, aren't you?"

Miguelito nodded. "There's lots we want to know."

The man laughed. "Yeah, kid. Me, too. Like sometimes I want to know what's the point?"

"Huh?" Miguelito and I said. Some grown-ups are really weird.

"Yeah, honey. *Huh?* That's what I say."

The man picked up the chair and took it inside. He never even told us if the new owners had kids.

We waited another minute. When no one else came out of the house, I glanced

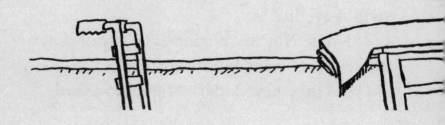

around. The house was dark and quiet. No one was looking.

"*Quédate quieto, Miguelito.*" I pried his fingers from mine. "Don't move."

I stepped to the back of the truck and peeked inside.

Way in the back were three bicycles: two big bikes and a small one.

And you won't *believe* this! The small one was just like mine.

Only it was pink and purple.

A girl's bike!

SOMETHING REALLY COOL!

"Hey, you guys!"

The next morning I ran into my third-grade classroom. I couldn't wait to tell my friends the news.

My best friends, Devin Suzuki and Jasmine Lange, turned in their seats.

We still had a few minutes before class started, and everyone was talking and goofing around. Some kids were sitting at their desks, some were standing.

"Where were you this morning?" Devin asked. Her light brown hair sparkled in the bright light. Jasmine must have slipped some glitter in it. Jazz always has fun stuff like glitter or clips for our hair.

"We gave up waiting for you." Jasmine's black hair was all glittery, too.

"Sorry." I slid into my seat. I sit right in front of Devin and next to Jasmine. We were lucky our teacher let us sit so close together. "I was running late, so Papi drove me."

Just then someone called out, "Hey, you guys!" in a high, screechy voice.

We turned. It was Johnny Wiley, my worst enemy and the major cause of my third-grade troubles.

¡Caracoles! Doggone it! He was making fun of me *again*!

Johnny stretched his nostrils with his fingers and made a pig face. But, trust me, it didn't take much of a stretch. It was most of the way there already.

I rolled my eyes. Johnny Wiley is the reason I changed my name. He kept saying I was a blabbermouth and called me Blabby Gabby. So I added the accent to Gabi and made it Gabí. Now it does NOT rhyme with *blabby* because I do NOT talk too much.

My toes curled in my sneakers. I wished I had my boots. When I wear my boots I feel like I can do anything!

But last month, I got in trouble for losing my temper and trying to kick Johnny. Then our teacher, Mr. Fine, said I could never wear my boots to school again. He even sent a note about it to my parents.

I bit my lip.

"Ignore him." Jasmine put her hand on my shoulder.

I gave Johnny my I'll-deal-with-you-later glare.

Then Devin winked at me. "Hey, Jasmine, where's the glitter?" she asked. "Gabí needs some, too."

I grinned. Devin can always make me feel better.

She's my very best friend. It feels like I've known her forever and we both speak Spanish. But Jasmine doesn't. So when Jasmine's not around, Devin and I speak Spanish as much as we can. That way, Devin can practice so she won't forget what she knows, and Jazz won't feel left out.

Devin screwed off the top of the glitter

22

bottle and peeked inside. "There's just enough. . . ."

She rubbed the inside of the cap with her finger. Then she dabbed a bit on my bangs.

I crossed my eyes and looked up. Sure enough, my bangs were all sparkly.

I smiled at Devin. She grinned so big that the braces on her front two teeth gleamed like the glitter in her hair. Then, quick as a blink, she put her hand in front of her mouth. She doesn't want her braces to show. Devin's really shy.

Then I remembered my big news. I couldn't believe I almost forgot to tell them!

"Oh, you won't *believe* this!" I said. "I have something *really* cool to tell you."

"What is it?" Jasmine and Devin shrieked at the same time. "Tell us!"

"Okay," I began. I told them all about the moving van, the new neighbors, and the three bikes.

"I think they have a girl our age!" I said.

"Lucky!" Jasmine said. "There aren't *any* kids on my street." Jasmine turned to Devin. "Isn't that cool, Dev?"

"I guess." Devin shrugged. "Have you met her? How come she's not in school?"

I shook my head. "They haven't moved in yet. But I definitely saw a girl's bike."

Devin snorted. "That doesn't mean anything. Maybe it's an old bike, and the girl's already grown-up. Or maybe they're just keeping the bike for someone. This new girl probably doesn't even exist."

I stared at Devin for a second. I'd never seen her so worked up. She's usually pretty quiet.

I glanced at Jasmine. She shrugged.

"I'll bet she does, too, exist!" I said. "And when I get home, I'll prove it!"

I stomped my foot. But stomping my sneaker didn't sound as good as stomping my boot.

"Well, even if she does exist," Devin said,

"how do you know she's going to be nice?
She could be snotty, like Sissy Huffer. You
could hate her."

The three of us turned to look at Sissy.
Sissy crinkled her nose and gave us a snooty
smile. Then she shook her yellow curls and
turned her back on us.

"See?" Devin said. "Your new neighbor
girl could be like *that*."

I stared at Devin. I didn't get it. Why was she suddenly acting so mean? She's never mean.

A funny look crossed Devin's face. But she wouldn't look me in the eye.

Before I could say anything else, Mr. Fine walked to the chalkboard.

I turned back to Devin. She looked past me toward Mr. Fine.

"This morning," said Mr. F, "we'll work on synonyms and antonyms."

His bushy eyebrows bounced above his glasses. That meant he was trying to make our new topic sound exciting. But it seemed like nothing could be more *boooring*!

How could synonyms and antonyms keep my mind off the new girl?

I sank down in my seat. It was going to be really hard to sit still all day.

I couldn't wait to get home!

CUATRO
CHAPTER 4
WHO'S THAT GIRL?

Right after school, I raced home to put on my cowgirl boots.

I was going to the haunted house to do some good old detective work. I want to be a secret agent when I get older. So I need all the practice I can get. And with any luck, I'd find some clues about the owner of the pink and purple bike.

If there really was a new girl, she might need a friend.

I yanked on my boots, gave Tippy a quick kiss behind his ears, and flew downstairs.

"Regreso pronto, Abuelita!" I yelled. Then

I ran out-
side and
down the
block.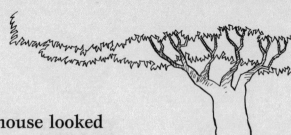

The old house looked
the way it always did, huge
and dark and creepy.

I ducked behind a mulberry
tree and waited. I started to
feel like a spy with a *top secret* mission.

I stooped down and crept for-
ward. I couldn't see anything moving across
the street. Nothing inside the house . . . or
outside. I was about to go home when I
thought I saw movement in the tower room.

A small face peered out. *Was I seeing
things?*

I climbed up the mulberry tree. Slowly, I
peeked through the branches.

After a few minutes, the front door
creaked open.

I held my breath.

A small head with long, black hair poked out. A pale face with big, dark eyes looked left, then right. Then a girl stepped onto the porch.

Who's that girl? Is that the new girl? Or is it . . . a ghost?

I could only see her head. The rest of her was hidden by potted plants and the porch rail. She looked about my height, so I figured she must be my age.

The moment I spotted her, our eyes met and she disappeared.

¡Caracoles! I thought. *Maybe she really is a ghost.*

I pushed away a few branches to get a better look.

She was kneeling at the edge of the porch, peeking around a tall post. She wore a plaid

skirt and
a white
blouse with
a necktie.

She saw me and
disappeared again. I won-
dered if I was really seeing her
or just imagining her. The skin on my arms
got all creepy-crawly with *carne de gallina*.
¡Un espíritu!

I thought about going home, but I remembered that in most ghost stories, the
ghost needs help. What kind of secret agent
would turn her back on someone who needs
help? Even if that someone is a ghost.

"Wait!" I slithered down the mulberry
tree. "Come back! I won't hurt you. I just
want . . . to make friends."

The pale face appeared again.

"Hi! Uh . . . I just live five houses
down." I pointed. "Over there. We're neighbors."

The girl blinked.

"Can I, uh, come over and talk?"

When she didn't say anything, I took a chance and crossed the street. I stopped at the bottom of the porch steps.

Escalofríos tickled the back of my neck. I tried to ignore the chills.

"Hi." I felt like I was talking to a stray kitty I didn't want to scare off. I took a deep breath. "Are you real?"

She tilted her head, like she wasn't sure what I meant.

I tried again. "Are you real or are you . . . a ghost?"

 She smiled and her face got all bright. Slowly, she reached down and touched me. Her fingers were warm and solid.

I let out the

breath I was holding and smiled back. *I've read* way *too many ghost stories.*

"My name's Gabí."

"I'm Lizzie," she said in a voice so soft I wasn't sure I heard her right.

"Lizzie?"

She nodded. "But some people call me Lizard." At the look on my face, she added, "Because I like to climb."

I grinned. "Lizard. I like that. I've got two names, too. I'm —"

"Lizzie!" A woman's voice called from inside. "Lizzie, where are you?"

Lizzie's eyes opened wide. "I have to go in. You'd better go, too."

"Oh, uh . . . can I come back tomorrow?" I asked.

Lizzie stared at me for a moment, then blinked. She nodded.

She was still stooped down on the porch floor, staring at me. I could tell she wasn't going to move until I left.

Was she hiding something? I wondered.

I waved and turned to go.

The moment I looked away, I heard the door slam.

When I turned back, she was gone.

I crossed the street and raced for home. My mind was racing, too.

Now I know who that girl is, I thought. *She's Lizzie, called Lizard.*

And she's a real, live girl.

Still, as Mami would say, *aquí hay un gato en saco.* There's a cat in the bag. That means something weird is going on. . . .

But what?

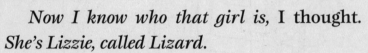

WHO DID THIS?

When I got back home, I flopped down on the couch in the family room to watch TV. But I couldn't stop thinking about Lizzie.

Our house was superquiet. Abuelita and Papi were in the backyard, working on the garden. Mami was upstairs in her office. Miguelito was out front, riding his trike.

Just then, the front door slammed.

"Waaaaaaahh! Gabi!Gabi!Gabííííííííí!"

Miguelito pounded down the hall and into the family room.

I jumped up and snapped off the TV. My

little brother was crying *a moco tendido*, as Mami would say. With snot hanging.

"*¿Qué pasó, Miguelito?*" I wiped his nose.

His face was all red and puffy. Tears streamed down his cheeks. He tried to talk, but he was blubbering so hard, I couldn't understand him.

"What happened, Miguelito?" I asked him again. Then I checked him over for scrapes and bruises. "Did you fall? You don't seem hurt."

"I was riding my trike." Miguelito pointed toward the front of the house. "They . . . they . . . they . . ." He started blubbering again.

"They who, Miguelito? Who did this to you? Did somebody hurt you? Tell me who it was. I'll fix them — I'll — I'll —" I started jumping and kicking and punching the air like a kickboxer.

"No! They're too big!"

"Who's too big?" I kicked and punched

again. "Nobody's going to make my little brother cry and get away with it. Who is it? Tell me. I'll — I'll —"

"They'll hurt you!" Miguelito sobbed.

That's when I remembered how my spunky feet always got me into trouble. And now my spunky feet were scaring my little brother. *I have to use my head and not my feet, like Papi always tells me.*

And tengo que dar buen ejemplo, I thought. *I have to set a good example for Miguelito, like Mami wants.*

I took a deep breath and knelt down beside my little brother.

"Okay, Kikito." (He likes it when I call him that.) *"Dime,* tell me, who did this?"

"Teenagers!" Miguelito covered his face with his hands and cried harder.

"Teenagers?"

That could mean *anybody* outside our family. Miguelito thinks anyone my age or older is a "teenager." And I'm only in third grade! To him, teenagers are so cool, he's afraid to look straight at them.

I stroked his hair. "Do I know them? Have you ever seen them before?"

Miguelito shook his whole body back and forth. I knew he meant "no."

"*Vay, vay*, Miguelito, there, there. *Cálmate*. Try to calm down. I need to know what they did to you."

Miguelito sniffled and lowered his hands. "They were mean. They said, 'Little kids have to pay a toll.' Then they wouldn't let me pass. And then I cried. And then . . . they laughed at me!"

Miguelito started howling again.

I bit my lower lip. My toes curled in my boots. I hated to see my little brother cry. But I had to hold my temper.

"*Vay*, Miguelito, listen carefully. Where were these teenagers when they were mean to you?"

Miguelito covered his face with his left

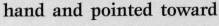

hand and pointed toward the front sidewalk with his right.

"Down the block? Were they near the new neighbors? No?"

Miguelito was only allowed to play on our side of the street. If the bullies weren't across from Lizzie's house, they must be on the other end of our block: up the hill, by the giant mulberry tree.

"Okay, Kikito," I said. "I'll take care of it. Go in the yard with Papi and Abuelita." I opened the sliding glass door for him.

Then I raced outside and flew up the street.

Ka-thump! Ka-thump! Ka-thump! My boots hit the sidewalk hard as I stomped up the hill.

I could practically feel the smoke coming out of my ears. Nobody makes my brother cry and gets away with it. *Nobody!*

I was aching to fix those bullies, but I knew I had to calm down.

How can I make them stop picking on Miguelito without using my spunky feet? I wondered. *Maybe I can talk to them. . . .*

I looked around for the bullies, but the sidewalk was deserted.

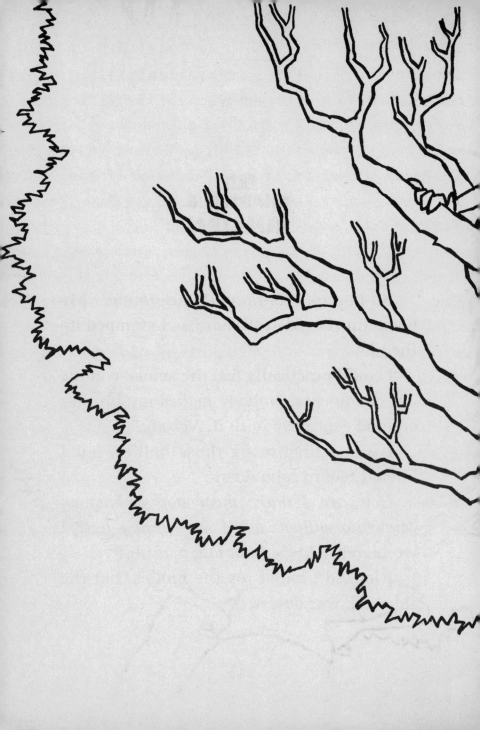

"They're around here somewhere," I muttered to myself.

Just as I stepped under the mulberry tree, I felt it shudder and shake. Then I heard a scraping sound, and . . .

You're not going to believe this! Two big boys jumped from the branches and landed *Thump! Thump!* on either side of me.

No wonder Miguelito was crying, I thought. *These bullies are big!*

But they're not scaring me! With my boots on, I feel just as big as them!

I stood tall with my fists on my hips and my boots pointed out.

They took a step forward.

First Bully: "Little kids can't —"

Second Bully: "— go past this line."

They pointed at a crack in the sidewalk.

"Hey!" I looked from one to the other. "Who're you calling a little —?"

That's when I noticed: The big nasty bullies looked exactly the same. Short, dark crew cuts. Round, red faces. They were even dressed in matching baggy T-shirts and droopy black shorts.

The bullies were twins. Bully Twins!

I took a deep breath and stepped between them, right over the crack.

I turned back to face them. They weren't that tall, but they were real beefy looking. They had to be fifth or sixth graders.

"I stepped over the line," I said. "What are you going to do about it?"

Their foreheads crinkled at the same time.

Left Twin: "We're going to make you —"

Right Twin: "— pay the toll."

They both stuck out their hands. "Fifty cents!" they said in one voice.

I stared at them for a second. Then I snorted.

"When frogs grow hair!" I said. "I'd rather drink dirt! I don't owe you *anything*! But *you* owe my little brother an apology."

Left Twin: "The little crybaby —"

Right Twin: "— on the plastic baby bike? And you're the crybaby's —"

Left Twin: "— *big* sister? Oh, we're really —"

Right Twin: "— scared!"

Then the Twins started shivering and shaking. They made scaredy-cat faces and hugged each other. They both kept saying, "I'm soooo scared!"

I couldn't stand it anymore. I stomped one boot.

"Stop it!" I yelled. "You're not funny! We've lived on this block all our lives. Nobody makes us pay a toll! *Nobody!*"

As I glared at the Twins, I remembered what Papi always said: "Use your head, not your feet." I was trying, I really was. But right now, my head was saying: "Use your feet!"

I stomped my other boot. I put my fists on my hips. "You'd better stop picking on my brother!"

The Twins looked at each other for a second and totally cracked up. Then they started stomping their feet and doing a tap dance on the sidewalk. It was like they had planned it ahead of time.

The Twins bounced all around me, so I couldn't tell which was Right Twin or which was Left Twin. They giggled like the hyenas in *The Lion King*.

I stomped my boot again. "Stop it, I said! *Stop it!Stop it!Stop it!*"

They jumped away and hugged each other again, pretending to look scared.

First Twin: "*Ooo-ooo!* What are you going to do?"

Second Twin: "Tap dance us to death?"

First Twin: "Or maybe beat us in a hoedown?"

Second Twin: "No, no! She's going to line dance on our toes!"

They turned to each other and high-fived. They snickered and smirked.

I bit my lip. I'd always thought Johnny Wiley was one of the great evils of the universe. But the Bully Twins had him beat. *They* were the *greatest* evil.

My toes curled in my boots. I was *so* angry, I was giving off sparks. *Echaba chispas,* as Mami would say.

"You want to know what I'm going to do?" I told them. "*Here's* what I'm going to do!"

I kicked up my feet, did some awesome kickboxing moves, and spun around to face them. But before I could get closer, both boys fell down under the mulberry tree. They rolled and sputtered on the grass.

I stared at them.

¡Caracoles! I stomped my boot so hard that sharp tingles shot up my leg.

You *won't* believe this! They were laughing at me.

How humiliating!

SIETE
CHAPTER 7
MAKING FRIENDS

"A ghost?" Jasmine bounced beside me like Miguelito.

The next day after school, Jazz, Devin, and I headed straight to Lizzie's house. I hoped Lizzie wouldn't mind that I'd brought my friends with me. I didn't know much about Lizzie, but I had a feeling we'd all make good friends. And I just couldn't wait for Devin and Jazz to meet her.

"You didn't tell me you thought she was a ghost." Devin sounded like she'd caught me cheating at checkers.

Right away, I felt bad. "I'm sorry I didn't

tell you, but she's *not* a ghost. Her name is Lizzie. And she's new here, so she needs friends."

"You're *sure* she's not a ghost?" Jasmine made her pouty face. "She *does* live in a haunted house."

"*Shhh*, she'll hear us." I knocked on the front door.

But before I stopped knocking, the door opened. Lizzie's face peeked out.

"Hi, Lizzie. I brought my friends to meet you. This is Devin, and this is Jasmine." I stepped away so she could see them.

"Oh!" Lizzie looked a little scared — like I'd told her to speak on stage in her underwear, or something.

"Uh," I began, "maybe we could hang out together?"

Lizzie gulped. "Um, okay. But first, I have to change clothes."

All I could see were Lizzie's head and shoulders through the door. She was wear-

ing the white blouse, necktie, and plaid skirt again. Maybe it was a school uniform.

"I'll meet you in the backyard," she said. Without waiting for an answer, Lizzie closed the door.

We heard her thump away.

"I wonder why she didn't open the door?" I said.

Jazz crossed her eyes and grinned. "Maybe it's because the house really *is* haunted." She jumped down the porch steps. "Come on! Let's check out the back."

"Devin?" I said. "Are you coming?"

Devin was staring at her feet. "Maybe I should go home. You've got Jasmine and the new girl to hang out with. . . ."

Devin has always been a little afraid to make new friends.

"Hurry up, you guys!" Jasmine called. She was already at the corner of the house.

"Devin," I said, "please stay. It won't be the same without you."

It took almost forever for us to talk her into it, but Devin finally agreed to stay.

When we got to the backyard, Jasmine gasped. "Wow! What is that word you guys say all the time?"

"Chévere," Devin and I said. It means "very cool."

The three of us stood there staring. The backyard was a kid's dream come true.

A huge redwood jungle gym ran across half the lawn. It had ladders and swings and monkey bars and rings. At the top was a small wooden platform with rails all around. A humongous green plastic tube wound around the whole thing. I was itching to slide through that tube!

A redwood fort stood in one corner of the yard.

In another corner, tucked between two tall pine trees, sat the coolest little playhouse! It would make the perfect clubhouse for three or four girls, just like Devin, Jasmine, Lizzie, and me.

"Double *chévere*!" Jasmine ran toward the jungle gym. We followed.

"Hi!" said a voice from high up on the jungle gym.

A sheet of black hair slid down from the wooden platform at the top of the gym. A pale face followed. Lizzie was already outside.

She turned a quick somersault and hung from a bar by her legs. She had changed into long blue jeans and a plain white T-shirt.

Lizzie did a fancy flip, jumped down, and landed on one foot.

She turned to Devin and Jazz. "Hi. I'm Lizzie. I like to climb. Wanna join me?"

Lizzie zipped back up the bars and did a belly flip. She seemed different than when she was on the porch or peering through a window. She was much friendlier now.

"Hey, you really are as quick as a lizard," I called up to her.

"Yeah, that was a really good dismount you did a little while ago." Jasmine followed Lizzie up the bars. "Do you take gymnastics?"

"Not yet. I will, though. As soon as, uhhh . . . as soon as my mom can set it up."

"You seem like a natural," Jasmine said. She had been taking tumbling and gymnastics since she was in first grade. "Maybe you can take lessons from my coach."

"Maybe." Lizzie hung upside down again. "We'll see."

I looked at the big house behind us. "Hey, Lizzie," I said, "um, is your house *really* haunted?"

"I haven't seen any ghosts yet," she said, swinging upside down. "Other than me, that is."

Everyone laughed and Lizzie gave me a big goofy, upside-down grin.

I felt my ears get warm, but I laughed, too. I remembered Lizzie's smile yesterday when I asked her if she was a ghost. She was nice not to laugh at me.

Then Lizzie taught me some cool tricks, while Devin watched. Devin seemed extra shy. But Lizzie kept talking to her, so Devin finally loosened up and joined us.

When Lizzie and Jazz started to show off for each other, Devin and I checked out the playhouse.

The playhouse was small and dark inside. It smelled of sweet wood. A long bench with a cushion on it took up the whole left wall. And a small table with four chairs sat in the middle of the room.

"This is so cool!" Devin said as we stepped inside.

"Isn't it?" I sat at one of the tiny chairs. "Lizzie seems nice."

"Yes, but . . ." Devin sat on the bench.

"But what?"

"She's kind of strange, *¿no crees?*" Devin's forehead crinkled. "I get the feeling she's hiding something."

"*Sí, creo que sí.*" I switched to Spanish so Lizzie wouldn't overhear. "But I haven't figured out what."

I remembered how mysterious Lizzie was acting when I first met her. And how today, she wouldn't open the door.

"Umm . . . Gabí," Devin began, "now that Lizzie lives right down the block from you . . . are you going to stop hanging out with me?"

I stared at her. "*¿Qué?* Is *that* why you've been acting so weird?"

"It's just . . ." Devin looked away. "I was

afraid you'd like Lizzie so much you'd stop liking me. I'd just die if you didn't want to be my friend anymore."

"Are you kidding?" My jaw dropped. "You're my best friend. You'll always be my best friend. No matter how many friends I have. Ever."

Devin looked up. Her eyes were all watery. "Really?"

"*¡Claro que sí!* Of course!" I stomped my foot. "Would Gabí the Great ever lie?"

Devin smiled big enough to show her braces. Then real quick, she hid them again.

Friendship is a tricky business, I thought. *I may have to be more careful with other people's feelings.*

We heard laughing and running. Then the door opened.

"Don't you guys want to play on the bars anymore?" Jasmine poked her head in and looked around. "Oh, very *chévere*!"

"Go on in, Jasmine." Lizzie was standing

behind her. "I *think* there's room for all of us."

Jasmine sat down next to Devin. When Lizzie hopped up the two front steps and into the house, she tripped.

"You okay?" Jasmine jumped up to catch her before she fell.

"Oh, yeah." Right away, Lizzie's face got pink. But she swished her hair in front of it so no one would see.

Lizzie sat across from me at the little table. "There's a loose floorboard I forgot about. I always trip there."

I looked at the floor. I didn't see anything to trip on. But I didn't say anything.

Instead, I said, "This place is really cool. Have you ever used it as a clubhouse?"

Lizzie shook her head. "There weren't any girls my age near our last house. And my school was pretty far from home."

"Oh, will you be going to our school now?" Jasmine asked.

"Nuh-uh. I go to a private school — St. Rita's."

"I've heard of St. Rita's," Devin said. "Isn't it . . . oh . . ."

"It's for kids with learning disabilities." Lizzie finished Devin's sentence.

Devin nodded. "I know. My cousin Bobby goes there. He has dyslexia. He switches around letters a lot. Numbers, too. It makes it hard for him to read."

"Me, too." Lizzie smiled. "St. Rita's is actually a fun school. There are lots of really smart kids there. We just learn in a different way than other kids. The problem is I still don't live near my school friends."

"That's a bummer," I said. Then I smiled. "But now you live close to us."

"Yeah!" said Jazz and Devin together.

Then Devin looked at me and smiled so big her braces showed. This time, she didn't even try to cover them up.

OCHO
CHAPTER 8
BROTHERS, SUPERHEROES, AND SPUNKY FEET

The next day, Lizzie and I were playing on her jungle gym again. But this time we were alone. Jazz had gymnastics and Devin's mom wanted her to go straight home.

Lizzie climbed up and touched a white star on the side of my red boot.

"I love your boots," she said.

I lifted my right boot so she could see it better. "My *papi* says I have spunky feet. My boots and my spunky feet are my secret weapons. They make me feel strong. And they help me stand up to bullies and bad guys. But sometimes they get me into trouble." I told her all about the mess with Johnny Wiley.

Lizzie sucked on a strand of hair for a moment. "You know, I fight bad guys, too."

"You do?" *¡Caracoles!* I thought. *This girl is full of surprises!*

"Yup. C'mon, I'll show you." Lizzie slithered down the bars and ran to the playhouse. I followed.

"Look." She pulled a sketch pad from inside the bench and showed me.

"I can't believe it! You drew Dragon-Ella!" I sat on the bench. "She's my favorite superhero."

"No way! She's mine, too!" Lizzie said. "I've been practicing drawing her so I can get good enough to draw my own superhero comics. See?" Lizzie flipped the page.

A girl in a black leotard filled the page. The leotard had a big green lizard painted on the front. The girl was jumping from one tall building to the next.

"This is Gecko Girl." Lizzie sat next to me. "I made her up."

"Really?" I glanced at Lizzie. "Uhh . . . if I tell you something, do you swear you won't tell anyone else?"

Lizzie crossed her heart, zipped her lips, locked them, and tossed away the key.

I smiled and scooted closer to her. "When I get older, I'm going to be the head of a secret government agency, like the CIA. I want to fight bad guys. So, umm . . . I sort of made up my own superhero, Gabí the Great. She's like Gecko Girl. But I can't draw her."

I glanced at Lizzie to see if she was going to laugh. She leaned forward, like she wanted to hear more. But she didn't even crack a smile. So I went on.

"Only my friends and family know that I'm really into crime fighting, though. Some of the kids at school would make fun of me if they knew. So you can't tell *anybody*."

Lizzie pointed at her zipped, locked lips.

"Good." I nodded.

"Gecko Girl fights bad guys, too." Lizzie turned to me. "You know what a gecko is?"

"Sure, it's a quick little lizard." I grinned. "They have them in Puerto Rico, where my mom and grandma are from."

"Yup, a quick little lizard," she said. "You know what's cool about Gecko Girl?"

I shrugged. "What?"

"She loves to climb, like me. Then she lost her leg in a mountain-climbing accident and now she has a bionic leg. It has super-human strength and it's her secret weapon. But nobody can tell 'cause it looks just like the other leg. See?"

I nodded as I gazed down at the drawing of Gecko Girl. "I wish I could draw this well."

"I wish I could wear cool boots like yours," Lizzie said. She tucked her feet under the bench, hiding her big leather sneakers. "Someday I'll have supercool boots 'cause I have spunky feet like you. Watch."

Lizzie ran back outside and zipped up

one row of monkey bars and down another. She really did remind me of a lizard. A lizard with spunky feet.

I climbed up after her. "Hey, Lizzie. Who calls you Lizard?"

"My brothers. And sometimes my dad." Lizzie did a somersault.

"You have brothers?" I sat on the wooden platform at the top of the jungle gym.

"Yup, two older brothers." Lizzie climbed up and sat next to me. "They're really nice and all, but they're way too protective. They think because I'm . . . uh . . . younger than them, I'm going to fall and hurt myself. They treat me like a wimp. I *hate* that! They always yell at me when I climb too high. I'd rather play alone."

I nodded. "I kind of know how they feel. I have a little brother, and I yell at him when I think he does dangerous things."

"Yup," she said, "and if someone else tries to hurt me, watch out!"

"Same here!" I sat up on my knees. "There were these two mean bullies picking on my little brother the other day. And I let them have it!"

I stood on the platform and did a few kickboxing moves. "Just like that!"

Lizzie jumped to the ground so I could show off a few more kicks, when —

"Hey, Lizard!" A boy's voice called from the side of the house.

Then — you won't believe this!— two identical, beefy twins ran into the yard.

When we spotted one another, all three of us froze: I had one boot in the air. They had matching grins.

First Twin: "Hey, Lizard, what are you doing with —"

Second Twin: "— the cowgirl line dancer?"

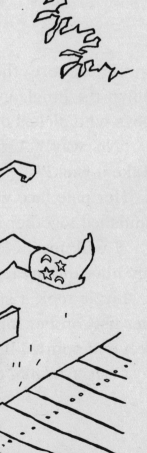

NUEVE
CHAPTER 9
LIAR!

"Those are the bullies!" I scrambled down the jungle gym. "Those are the mean boys who picked on my little brother!"

"No way!" Lizzie said. "It's not true! Take it back!"

Her pale face was all red. Her eyebrows squished together in a frown.

"I will not!" I faced her with my fists on my hips and my legs apart.

Lizzie took a step toward me and stuck her fists on her hips, too. She glanced at my feet and pointed her toes out just like mine.

Gecko Girl and Gabí the Great face off!

"You'd better," she said, "'cause it's a big, fat *lie*! Jack and Jake are my brothers. They would never be mean to anybody. *Ever!*"

My eyes slid over to the chunky twins who stood behind her.

They smirked. They waved their fingers. They even winked at me.

My neck got all hot. I was so mad sparks flew! *¡Echaba chispas!*

"Look!" I pointed. "They're making fun of me, right now!"

Lizzie turned. Her brothers stared back at her with sad, puppy-dog eyes.

First Twin: "She picked on us."

Second Twin: "She tried to kick us."

Lizzie looked down at my boots. "So that's why your boots get

you in trouble. You pretend nice boys are bad guys, then you try to kick them."

I almost choked. "What? No! Your brothers made my little brother cry! They tried to boss me around, too."

She stared at me and shook her head. "I thought you were my friend. But all you are is a liar!"

I felt like she'd slapped me. What a mean thing to say!

"I am *not* a liar!" I said. "I'm telling the truth!" I stomped my boot.

Lizzie scrunched up her eyes. Her lips turned into a thin white line.

"Maybe you should go home," she said, pointing toward the side gate.

I gulped past the brick that had lodged in my throat. I felt as bad as I did when my first cat died. I'd never been kicked out of someone's yard before. I tried to talk, but nothing would come out.

So I turned and left.

Just before I rounded the corner, I looked back. Lizzie was still watching me, but the corners of her mouth were turned down. She looked as sad as I felt.

Behind her, the Bully Twins grinned and waved. Then they held up their thumbs and winked.

I turned and ran. I reached home just as hot tears fell.

Who knew making friends could be so hard!

DIEZ
CHAPTER 10
FRIENDSHIP CAN HURT

"*Gabita, ¿qué pasó?*" Papi asked.

As I ran into my house, I bumped into Papi. I pushed my face against his chest.

"What's going on?" Papi repeated. He scooped me up in his arms.

I wrapped my arms and legs around him, like I used to when I was little. Then I buried my face in his neck. He didn't smell like lab chemicals today. He just smelled like Papi. I started to cry, loud and hard.

Mami and Abuelita ran in from the kitchen. "*¿Qué pasó?*" they asked.

I could feel Papi's shoulders shrug. *"No sé,"* he told them.

He carried me to the couch in the family room and set me down. Mami and Papi sat on either side of me. Abuelita pulled up a chair and sat in front of me.

"¿Te lastimaste?" Abuelita checked my arms and legs. "Are you hurt?"

I shook my head.

Mami slipped her arm around my shoulders and pulled me close.

Papi handed me a tissue. I was crying *a moco tendido* just like Miguelito.

When I finally stopped sobbing, I told them all about Lizzie, her bully brothers, and how she had called me a liar.

"But —" I started sniffling again. "— I really like her. She's usually really nice and she's fun. And she draws comics about superheroes. I've never had a friend who lived so close by."

Papi nodded. "Sounds like you have a lot in common. You both have spunky feet and you both love your brothers."

Papi's words made me start bawling. It felt like I'd lost Lizzie all over again. I had no idea friendship could hurt so much. But I knew I wanted Lizzie back as a friend.

"*Vay, vay,* Gabrielita, listen," Abuelita said. "Your *abuelito* always used to say, '*Amigo en la adversidad, amigo de verdad.*'"

"It's true," Mami said. "A friend who sticks by you in bad times is a *real* friend." She stroked my wavy hair. "I know Lizzie hurt your feelings," Mami went on, "but if you really want to be her friend, you won't give up on her. She loves her brothers, and she was doing what she thought was right."

Mami held my face and then kissed my forehead.

I thought about what Abuelito used to say. I sniffled and nodded. Lizzie may have hurt my feelings, but I was ready to be a real friend to her.

Even if it meant going back outside and making friends with the Bully Twins.

ONCE
CHAPTER 11
FOR LIZZIE

"No!No!No!" Miguelito yelled. "I don't want to pay a toll!"

"You have to," said a boy.

"Or you'll have to go back," said another.

I couldn't see the boys because they were up the hill, past the giant mulberry tree. But I could hear Miguelito.

"Noooo!" Miguelito started to cry.

I flew the rest of the way up the hill. I had gone back outside to find Jack and Jake. I was going to make friends with them for Lizzie. And there they were acting like the Bully Twins again. They towered over little

Miguelito, who was sitting on his trike, crying.

My jaw practically hit my chest. "I can't believe it!"

I stomped up to them. "You're still picking on little kids? *¡Caracoles!*"

The moment he heard my voice, Miguelito jumped off his trike and ran to me. He threw his arms around my waist and buried his face in my tummy.

First Twin: "*Cara*-what?"

Second Twin: "I think she said, 'Carob-cooties!'"

First Twin: "Is that anything like Hershey's Kisses?"

Second Twin: "I think she *likes* us!"

Both twins: "She wants to kiss us!"

My face felt like it had a mega-sunburn. "*Oowiii, yuck!* I'd rather kiss camel lips!"

The Twins turned into laughing hyenas, like they did when I first met them. The more they laughed, the more Miguelito cried.

I stroked his head. *"Vay, vay, no llores."* I told him not to cry. "Don't worry." I continued in Spanish, *"No te preocupes.* I'm here."

First Twin: "Blah, blah, blah, boo, boo?"

Second Twin: "Yah, goo, goo, boo, boo!"

The Twins went back and forth, talking gibberish. It took a few moments before I got it. They were making fun of my Spanish!

My ears got as hot as freshly fried *chicharrones* — pork rinds. Those *muchachos malos*! If I were Dragon-Ella with her laser gaze, I'd sizzle those bad boys like bacon!

Miguelito kept crying. I knelt down and whispered in his ear.

"Oo-oo! More goo-goo, blah-blah," both twins said at once. Then they really cracked up laughing.

Now *that* was just plain mean! It hurt my feelings, and it hurt my little brother's feelings, too. I stepped in front of Miguelito, hiding him behind me. He wrapped his arms around my waist.

I wanted to set a good example for Miguelito. I really did. But I didn't know what to do anymore. A big old lump in my throat made me want to cry, but no way would I let the Bully Twins see *that*.

So instead, I stomped my boot. Hard.

"Be quiet! Stop making fun of the way we talk. You're horrible! I can't believe I was trying to make friends with you, even if I was only doing it for Lizzie!"

First Twin: "Oo-oo! The little girlie-girl wanted to —"

Second Twin: "— make friends with us."

First Twin: "But now we —"

Second Twin: "— blew it!"

The Twins turned to each other, snorted, and screamed, "But who cares?"

"I do," said a small voice.

There was a rustling in the giant mulberry tree behind us. A pair of white leather sneakers topped by long baggy pants swung down to a low branch. Then a small body

followed them and
slid to the ground.

As she slid
down the trunk,
one of Lizzie's
pant legs got
stuck above
her knee. Lizzie
didn't notice. I
tried not to stare,
but I couldn't help
it. She was wearing a
plastic brace on the
bottom of her leg, just

below her knee. It was shaped like her leg
and stayed on with Velcro straps.

The cat just jumped out of the bag, I
thought. *El gato saltó del saco.*

DOCE
CHAPTER 12
YOU'RE NO WIMP!

"Gabí was right." Tears streamed down Lizzie's face, but her lips formed that thin white line.

"You guys *are* bullies." She walked toward her brothers. "Now you've made me lose the only neighborhood friend I've ever had. I wouldn't blame Gabí if she never talked to me again."

First Twin: "Aw, Lizard . . ."

Second Twin: ". . . don't be mad."

First Twin: "We're —"

Second Twin: "— sorry."

Lizzie marched forward until she was

standing in front of her beefy brothers. She looked like a mouse facing two elephants.

"You'd better be!" Lizzie shook her finger at them.

The Bully Twins took a step backwards.

Lizzie took another step forward. "But don't tell *me* you're sorry. Apologize to Gabí and her little brother. And promise you'll never pick on them again!"

Jack and Jake hung their heads. "We're sorry," they muttered.

"Louder," said Lizzie. "Look at them, and sound like you mean it."

The boys raised their eyes and looked at us. "We're sorry. We promise."

Then they turned to their sister. "Can we go now?"

Lizzie nodded. Then, as Mami would say, the Twins *pararon el rabo y cogieron el monte*. They lifted their tails and took to the hills. That means they ran like crazy.

Lizzie turned to me. "I'm sorry, too. I shouldn't have said all those mean things."

I shrugged and looked down. I didn't want her to see my watery eyes.

"It's okay," I said, "you were just standing up for your brothers. I would have done the same thing for Miguelito. Oh, I almost forgot —"

I pushed my little brother forward. "This is my little brother, Miguelito."

Lizzie smiled. "Hi, Miguelito. I'm Lizzie."

Miguelito covered his face with his hands, then he hid behind me again.

I rolled my eyes. "Miguelito's kind of shy around older kids."

Miguelito tugged my sleeve.

I patted his hand. *"Shhh, un momentito. I'm talking right now."*

Miguelito got all bouncy and antsy. Then he squatted down and duckwalked around me. He stopped in front of the brace on Lizzie's leg.

"Gabí, look," he said in English. "Lizzie has a boo-boo on her leg."

"Oh!" Real quick, Lizzie pushed down her pant leg, hiding the brace.

"Miguelito! Don't be rude!" I pulled him up. "Sorry, he's too little to know better."

"It's okay," Lizzie said. "I understand." But her cheeks had turned pink. I could tell she was embarrased.

"Is that why you can't wear boots or take gymnastics?" I asked. "And why you always wear long pants?"

Lizzie nodded. "But someday soon, I won't have to wear the brace anymore. That's why I climb so much. So I can make my leg stronger and prove to the doctors that I don't need a brace."

"Why do you have to wear it?" I asked.

"When I was born, my foot pointed the wrong way. I had a cast when I was a baby, to straighten it out. Now I have to wear a splint — that's this brace. It will help my leg and foot get straighter and stronger. I can walk without it now, but Dr. Dana wants me to keep wearing it a little longer. To make sure my foot doesn't get crooked again."

"Kind of like how Devin wears braces on her teeth to make them straight."

Lizzie nodded. "Kind of."

"It sort of makes your leg bionic," I said with a smile. "Like Gecko Girl."

"Yup." Lizzie nodded. "Bionic, just like Gecko Girl."

"And just like Gecko Girl, nobody knows about it," I said, "'cause it's hidden."

We started walking down the sidewalk, toward our houses. Miguelito walked next to me, hiding his head under my arm.

"Uh, Lizzie?" I said. "Why didn't you tell me about your brace?"

Lizzie shrugged. "I don't want people to treat me like a wimp, that's all."

I stopped. "You're no wimp! You're kind of scary when you're mad!"

Lizzie smiled real big. "So, can we still be friends?"

"¡*Caracoles!*" I said. "Of course!"

"I'm glad," said Lizzie.

"Me, too," I told her.

"Me, three!" Miguelito hopped out from under my arm.

But when Lizzie giggled, Miguelito jumped back and stuck his face against my side.

TRECE
CHAPTER 13
NEWEST FRIEND

A few days later, I was back at Lizzie's house. We were getting to be really good friends.

"Watch out, World!" I yelled from the top of Lizzie's green tube slide.

"Bad guys, beware!" Lizzie swung on a rope and landed at my side.

Me: "Gabí the Great!"

Lizard: "And Gecko Girl!"

"*Are heeeerrre!*" We both slid down the tube together.

Lizzie landed first and hopped out of the way. Then I flew out and jumped beside

Lizzie. We stood next to each other, as tall and straight as we could. Fists on our hips, feet apart.

Lizzie wore a short-sleeved black turtleneck and long black pants. Her black hair blew in the wind.

We turned to each other and high-fived. "Crime fighters, forever!"

Then Lizzie and I raced to our clubhouse.

As we closed the door, someone knocked.

"Just in time!" Lizzie said.

"Crime-fighting friends forever?" I whispered.

"Forever." Lizzie held up her pinkie, and I hooked mine to hers. It was our secret pledge.

"Anybody in there?" Jasmine knocked again.

"Gabí?" Devin called. "Lizzie?"

Lizard and I threw open the door.

I bowed and swished my hand around. "Welcome to the —"

"— Mulberry Street Clubhouse for Girls," said Lizard.

"Cool!" Jasmine hopped inside.

"*¡Chévere!*" Devin smiled and showed us her braces.

The four of us faced one another, stuck out our rears, and did a hip-wiggle dance. It was the signal that our first girls' club meeting had begun. After the meeting and a snack

of Abuelita's coconut cookies and guava juice, we ran out to play on the jungle gym.

I watched Lizzie zig and zag up and down the monkey bars.

I smiled. *Who's that girl?* I know who she is:

She's Lizzie, called Lizard.

Secret identity: Gecko Girl, my super-*amiga* in crime fighting.

And she's my newest friend.

Now I have *three* great friends! *Amigas de verdad.*

Friendship may be hard sometimes. But it's worth it.

I wouldn't give up *any* of my friends for *anything*!

¡HABLA ESPAÑOL!
(That means: *Speak Spanish!*)

abuelita (ah-booweh-LEE-tah): grandma

abuelito (ah-booweh-LEE-toh): grandpa

adversidad (ahd-veher-see-DAHD): bad times

ahora (ah-OH-rah): now

amigas (ah-MEE-gahs): friends who are girls

a moco tendido (ah MOH-koh tehn-DEE-doh):
with snot hanging; crying really hard

aquí (ah-KEE): here

bandido (bahn-DEE-doh): bandit

bien (beeyen): well; good; all right; okay

bien hecho (beeyen EH-cho): well done; very good

buen ejemplo (boowehn eh-HEM-ploh): good
example

cálmate (KAHL-mah-teh): calm down

camión (kah-MEEYOHN): truck

¡Caracoles! (kah-rah-KOH-lehs): snails; can
also be used to mean "Yikes!" or "Wow!" or
"Doggone it!"

carne de gallina (KAHR-neh deh gah-YEE-nah):
goosebumps

chévere (CHEH-beh-reh): cool!

chicharrones (chee-cha-RROH-nehs): pork rinds

chispas (CHEES-pahs): sparks

¡Claro que sí! (KLAH-roh keh SEE): Of course!

cogieron el monte (koh-HEEYEH-rohn ehl MOHN-teh): they took to the woods

Creo que sí (KREH-oh keh SEE): I believe so; I think so

de verdad (deh vehr-DAHD): real; true; or can mean really or truly

dime (DEE-meh): tell me

dos (dohs): two

es tarde (ehs TAHR-deh): it's late

escalofríos (ehs-kah-loh-FREE-ohs): chills; shivers

espíritu (ehs-PEE-ree-too): ghost

está bien (ehs-TAH beeyen): it's okay; it's all right

gato (GAH-toh): cat

la gran (lah grahn): the Great

malo (MAH-loh): bad

mami (MAH-mee): mommy

¡Mira! (MEE-rah): Look!

momentito (moh-mehn-TEE-toh): a little moment

muchachos (moo-CHAH-chohs): boys

mundo (MOON-doh): world

niños (NEE-nyohs): children

¿no crees? (noh KREH-ehs): don't you think so?

no llores (noh YOH-rehs): don't cry

no sé (noh SEH): I don't know.

no te preocupes (noh teh preh-oh-KOO-pehs): don't worry

papi (PAH-pee): daddy

¿Qué? (KEH): What?

¿Qué pasó? (KEH pah-SOH): What happened?

quédate quieto (KEH-dah-teh KEEYEH-toh): don't move

regreso pronto (reh-GREH-soh PROHN-toh): I'll be back soon.

saco (SAH-koh): bag

saltó (sahl-TOH): jumped

silencio (see-LEHN-seeyoh): silence; quiet

¡Te agarré! (teh ah-gah-RREH): I got you!

¿Te lastimaste? (teh lahs-tee-MAHS-teh): Are you hurt?

vay, vay (by, by): A comforting sound similar to saying "there, there" or "it's okay"

#3 No More Spanish!

No! No! NO! Gabí will not speak any more Spanish. EVER! She used to think being able to speak two languages was SO cool. But lately when she speaks Spanish, Gabí mixes up her words, she gets made fun of, and she gets in trouble. It's strike three and Spanish is out!

No es problema, right? WRONG. Gabí's *abuelita* (that's her grandma) doesn't understand English. Now Gabí has to *hablar español*, or miss out on all the family fun! She just doesn't have a choice . . . or does she?